W9-BYW-604

PRESENTED TO

WITH LOVE FROM

DATE

Jane Yolen *and* Heidi E.Y. Stemple
Illustrated by Matt Phelan

A KITE FOR MOON

ZONDERKIDZ

A Kite for Moon

This title is also available as a Zondervan ebook.

Requests for information should be addressed to:
Zonderkidz, *3900 Sparks Dr. SE, Grand Rapids, Michigan 49546*

ISBN 978-0-310-75642-2

Art direction: Ron Huizinga

Printed in China

19 20 21 22 23 /DSC/ 22 21 20 19 18 17 16 15 14 13 12 11 10 9 8 7 6 5 4 3 2 1

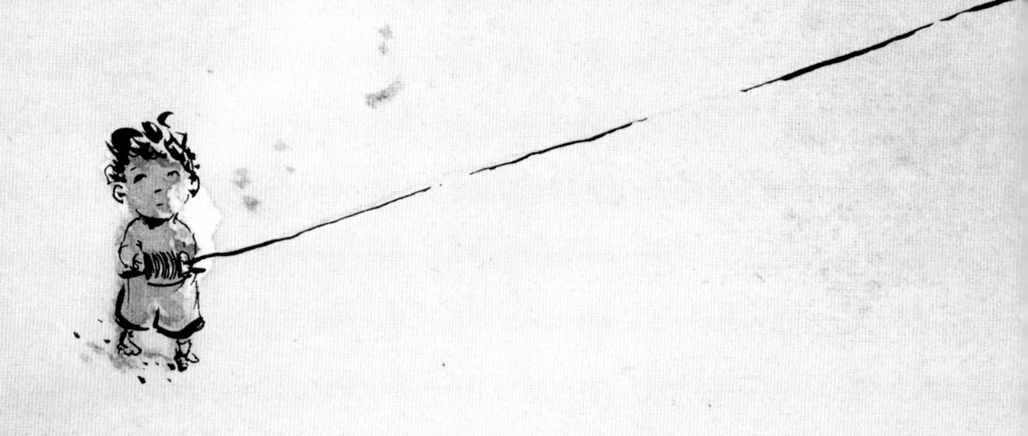

For Neil Armstrong,
who showed us the way.

It was morning and Moon sat alone in the sky.

The stars were all abed.

No one below was singing to her.

No one was sending up rockets

or writing poems about her.

No one was taking her photograph

or painting her picture.

Moon began to feel terribly sorry for herself.

Down below, a very small boy

flying his kite on the beach near his house,

looked up at Moon.

"Moon!" he called up to her. "Don't be sad!"

He ran as far as he could,

all the way to the edge of the water

where Moon sat on the horizon.

He tried to hug Moon

as his mother did to him

whenever he was unhappy.

But Moon was too far away.

So he wrote on his kite,

promising to come some day for a visit.

Then he let go

of his kite,

sending it up, up, up for Moon.

Days went by, years.

Moon waxed and waned.

She counted shooting stars and meteors.

She worried about peace down on earth

and strange objects whizzing by.

She eclipsed.

Many nights the boy watched Moon through a telescope

his father had given him.

Many days he sent up a new kite for Moon:

red kites, blue kites, green kites, yellow.

Some fell back to Earth,

some disappeared into the sky.

And Moon watched the boy grow.

Every day the boy studied hard.

He learned his large numbers

and his small sums.

He learned algebra and equations.

He learned geometry

and tried to square the circle.

He learned all about the sky

and the moon.

HAPPY
BIRTHDAY

He learned to ride a bicycle, drive a car, fly a plane and a rocket.

Then one day, when
he had learned
enough,

he went up, up, up

in a big rocket ship
with a fiery tail.

"Hello, Moon," he said. "I've come for that visit."

And the whole world watched.